The Potato Chip Champ

Discovering Why Kindness Counts

Written by
Maria Dismondy

Illustrated by
Dawn Beacon

Copyright ©2012 Maria Cini Dismondy
Illustrations by Dawn Beacon
Book Design by Kelsey Oseid

Second printing 2018
Printed in CHINA

Summary: Walter and Champ are two very different children. Walter teaches Champ a valuable lesson by giving up something that means a lot to both of them. Walter shows Champ what is truly important: sharing, empathy and kindness.

The Potato Chip Champ: Discovering Why Kindness Counts

ISBN 13: 978-0-9848558-1-0

Library of Congress Control Number: 2012912324

Cardinal Rule Press
An imprint of Maria Dismondy Inc.
5449 Sylvia
Dearborn, MI 48125
www.CardinalRulePress.com

BEFORE READING:

* Look at the cover illustration together. Ask your child if they know what a 'champ' is.

* Suggest a conversation about why kindness counts.

DURING READING:

* Talk about the word empathy and see if you can find examples of it in the book.

* Ask, Why do you think Champ lied about how many boxes of potato chips he sold?

AFTER READING:

* Why do you think Walter had so many friends and was well liked in the story?

* "It's not about what we have, but who we are." What does this theme from the book mean?

ADDITIONAL LEARNING:

* Try making homemade potato chips with your child.

* Create a taste test for the entire family of different kinds of chips. Make it fun with unique flavors like pickle chips and waffle & chicken flavored chips!

Dedicated to
my sister Angela.

She has a generous heart
and shares everything
from clothes to pickle
potato chips!

Champ loved potato chips. He ate them on his sandwiches. He crumbled them over his mac and cheese. He mixed them together with ice cream. Champ even dipped chocolate-covered potato chips in ranch dressing. If only his parents would let him eat them all the time!

There was only one thing Champ liked more than eating potato chips, and that was playing baseball. He was a good player and he knew it. Everything would have been perfect, except that Walter was on the team...

Walter Norbert Whipplemoore to be exact.

He was always late for practice, his shoes were dirty, he rode an old broken-down bike, and his name was too long to fit on his jersey. Walter was different, but the players on the team all liked him. Except for Champ, who had a hard time figuring out why.

Champ was shocked when he heard Coach announce the unusual fundraiser one day at practice. Champ knew he had to be the winner because the grand prize was a truckload of potato chips! All he had to do was sell the most boxes of chips to win.

Champ noticed Walter was getting more hits than anyone else at practice that day. Everyone but Champ cheered for Walter. Champ rolled his eyes and groaned.

After Walter left, Champ met up with Tommy, the catcher.

"Did you see how rusty Walter's bike is?" he sneered.

Tommy barked back, "You just don't like him because he plays better than you, and he has more friends, too."

At school, the boys talked about the fundraiser.

"I sold five boxes at karate," cheered Tommy.

"I sold ten boxes," lied Champ.

"Hey, Walter, you like chips too; how are you doing?" asked Tommy.

"I'm doing okay. I don't have as much time to sell the chips because I have a paper route," Walter added.

Answering with a mouthful of dill pickle chips, Champ mumbled, "Well, I plan on winning. They call me 'Champ' for a reason."

When Champ broke his leg sliding into home plate, he was devastated. He couldn't play ball for the rest of the season and would miss playing in the big game.

Champ was so bored. He really missed playing baseball and seeing his friends. He started making up games by nibbling on his chips and making letters out of them. Just as he was making the letter "C" out of a barbecue chip, there was a knock at the door. Champ peeked out the window. "Oh, it's Walter," he sighed.

Walter was shivering from the cold rain. "Hi, Champ, I brought over some cards. I heard you like to play," said Walter.

"Sure, if you *really* want to," Champ answered, wishing anyone but Walter had come over.

"Hey, why did you ride your bike here?" Champ asked.

"Oh, it's just me and my mom. We either take the bus or I have to ride my bike."

Champ couldn't believe what he was hearing. Walter was the only kid he knew whose mom didn't have a car. He thought about how hard that would be to have to ride your bike everywhere.

It was the night of the championship game and Walter made the winning hit. Champ wasn't sure which was worse — sitting on the bench, or finding out his dream of winning the truckload of potato chips was over. They announced over the loudspeaker that the winner was Walter Norbert Whipplemoore.

Champ moped around school the next couple of days.
Even his favorite tomato-flavored chips didn't cheer him
up. Could anyone love chips as much as he did? Champ
still wondered why the prize went to someone like Walter
and not him.

Walter Norbert Whipplemoore. He had a name longer than the Mississippi River and it didn't bother him at all.

When Champ got home from school on Friday, there was a huge truck parked in his driveway. Unloading box after box of chips were Coach and Walter.

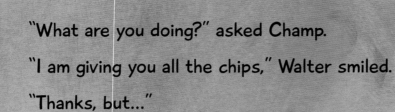

"What are you doing?" asked Champ.

"I am giving you all the chips," Walter smiled.

"Thanks, but..."

Before Champ could finish, Walter spoke. "Look, I'm crazy about chips too but you couldn't play ball and it's hard to sell boxes of chips with a broken leg. I know what it's like to really want something. I want you to have the chips."

"But...but...I don't deserve them," Champ stuttered.
Right then, Champ looked around his garage and saw a
brand new bike, two skateboards, a scooter, and fancy
rollerblades. How come he didn't see it before? He felt a
tightening in his chest. Champ had so much, why did he
always want more? Standing there in front of Walter was
really hard. Walter didn't have anything but an old, rusty
bike.

"Alright, we can split them, but I am not leaving here with all these chips!" laughed Walter.

"Deal!" answered Champ. "You know, Walter, *you're* the one they should call 'Champ' because being a champ isn't about having the nicest things. It's all about who you are. No wonder you have so many friends!"

The boys shook hands and that marked the beginning of a new friendship.

Maria Dismondy is a #1 best-selling children's book author, former teacher, and a highly sought-after speaker. She is also a self-proclaimed potato chip fan. Maria has a passion for spreading an anti-bullying message. With this most recent book, *The Potato Chip Champ*, she hopes to develop important character traits in children. She lives in southeastern Michigan with her husband, Dave, where they are raising three future potato chip lovers. To find out more about Maria and her award-winning books, visit www.mariadismondy.com

Illustrator Dawn Beacon lives with her husband and son in the beautiful mountains of Colorado. During the winter months she loves snowboarding with her family at their local resorts, while summertime finds her biking and gardening. Inspiration for her artwork is found directly out her back door with the abundance of wildlife and breathtaking views of the Vail Valley. Visit Dawn Beacon online at www.dawnbeacon.com.

Information for Families
by Barbara Gruener

Respect is about using good manners, being considerate of others' feelings, solving problems nonviolently, and treating others like we want to be treated. Teach your children to use the Golden Rule as a filter for their behaviors. Role-play scenarios to help them understand how respect looks, sounds, and feels. Then practice, practice, and practice some more.

Empathy, the ability to put oneself in others' shoes and feel what they're feeling, is an important virtue that we can elevate in our children. Use pictures, film clips, news stories, or real life experiences. Make it a point to discuss how people are feeling. Ask how people are feeling. Imagine how people are feeling. Try to switch roles with them to feel what they're feeling.

Responsibility is all about choices, consequences, and chores. Parents, let children make some decisions! Children learn to make good choices by doing it. Let them know up front that choices have consequences, both positive and negative. Encourage your children to consider the stakeholders (the people who might be affected by your choices) when they make their decisions. Let them know you're there if they mess up. Oh, and make sure they have some chores that they can be responsible for; it'll help strengthen their work ethic.

Integrity is all about doing the right thing. How can we teach integrity? First, we have to teach right from wrong by modeling what we do want and not permitting what we don't want. Developmentally, it's appropriate to give incentives and praise to our littlest learners as they make good choices. But as they grow older, we want them to do what's right just because it's right. Encourage students to let this question be their guide: Am I in the right place at the right time doing the right thing?

Forgiveness is the gift you give not only to someone else but also to yourself. Children will learn to forgive when they see you forgive. Try this: Put a few old potatoes in a sack and ask your child to carry them around everywhere they go for a week or so. Not only will that be a major inconvenience, but they'll eventually start to rot. Discuss how that parallels holding a grudge and refusing to forgive. Then role-play a good apology and teach them to say out loud and often, "I forgive you."

Barbara Gruener, counselor and character coach, works at a National School of Character. During her thirty years as an educator, Barbara has learned to appreciate that every child is a story waiting to be told. She lives in Friendswood, Texas, with her husband and their three children. Visit her online at www.corneroncharacter.blogspot.com